D0651258

Through a Glass Darkly

Bill Myers

HARBINGERS 17

Jeff Gerke, Angela Hunt and Alton Gansky

Published by Amaris Media International in conjunction with CreateSpace.

Copyright © 2016 Bill Myers

Cover Design: Angela Hunt

Photo credits: ©cvalli_111@fotolia.com

ISBN-13: 978-1540510099
ISBN-10: 1540510093

For more information, visit us on Facebook:
https://www.facebook.com/pages/Harbingers/70510730 9586877

or www.harbingersseries.com.

HARBINGERS

A novella series by
Bill Myers, Frank Peretti, Angela Hunt,
Alton Gansky, and Jeff Gerke

In this fast-paced world with all its demands, the four of us wanted to try something new. Instead of the longer novel format, we wanted to write something equally as engaging but that could be read in one or two sittings—on the plane, waiting to pick up the kids from soccer, or as an evening's read.

We also wanted to play. As friends and seasoned novelists, we thought it would be fun to create a game we could participate in together. The rules were simple:

Rule #1
Each of us would write as if we were one of the characters in the series:

Bill Myers would write as Brenda, the street-hustling tattoo artist who sees images of the future.

Frank Peretti would write as the professor, the atheist ex-priest ruled by logic.

Jeff Gerke would write as Chad, the mind reader with devastating good looks and an arrogance to match.

Angela Hunt would write as Andi, the brilliant-but-geeky young woman who sees inexplicable patterns.

Alton Gansky would write as Tank, the naïve, big-hearted jock with a surprising connection to a healing power.

Rule #2

Instead of the five of us writing one novella together (we're friends, but not crazy), we would write it like a TV series. There would be an overarching storyline into which we'd plug our individual novellas, with each story written from our character's point of view.

If you're keeping track, this is the order:

Harbingers 1—*The Call*—Bill Myers
Harbingers 2—*The Haunted*—Frank Peretti
Harbingers 3—*The Sentinels*—Angela Hunt
Harbingers 4—*The Girl*—Alton Gansky

Volumes 1-4 omnibus: Cycle One: *Invitation*

Harbingers 5—*The Revealing*—Bill Myers
Harbingers 6—*Infestation*—Frank Peretti
Harbingers 7—*Infiltration*—Angela Hunt
Harbingers 8—*The Fog*—Alton Gansky

Volumes 5-8 omnibus: Cycle Two: *The Assault*

Harbingers 9—*Leviathan*—Bill Myers
Harbingers 10—*The Mind Pirates*—Frank Peretti
Harbingers 11—*Hybrids*—Angela Hunt
Harbingers 12—*The Village*—Alton Gansky

Volumes 9-12 omnibus: Cycle Three: *The Probing*

Harbingers 13—*Piercing the Veil*—Bill Myers
Harbingers 14—*Home Base*—Jeff Gerke
Harbingers 15—*Fairy*—Angela Hunt
Harbingers 16—*The Sea*—Alton Gansky

Volumes 13-16 omnibus: Cycle Four: *The Pursuit*

Harbingers 17—*Through a Glass Darkly*—Bill Myers

There you have it, at least for now. We hope you'll find these as entertaining in the reading as we did in the writing.

Bill, Frank, Angie, Al, and Jeff

THROUGH A GLASS DARKLY

"We will be arriving at Baghdad International Airport in approximately twenty minutes. Please return to your seats, stow your tray tables, and put away any articles you may have removed during flight. Electronic devices must be turned off at this time."

I glanced up from my sketchpad and looked out the window. Nothing but brown. Brown hills, brown mountains, brown deserts. Same brown I'd seen the last two hours. I shook my head and went back to sketching.

The rest of the team, Cowboy, Andi, and Pretty Boy sat up in the other compartment, which was fine with me. We'd been on the outs since we got word of our little trip a couple nights back. I suppose you could blame me, but you gotta admit I had a pretty good argument.

It's not that I got somethin' against where we're

heading . . . 'cept for the fact somebody's always blowing somebody up—Iraq, Iran, or wherever we're goin'. I'm no geography major and don't care 'bout the details, but it's like every day you hear bad stuff happening there.

Not exactly the place to be dragging a kid, no matter how important our assignment. Then there's the stuff the professor told us when he dropped in for a guest appearance from that other universe or dimension or wherever he is:

"Every battle has been a prelude to the war
that must come. The war you must win."

Nope. Not with my boy. I don't care how much they guilt me. Daniel's my responsibility and I'm calling the shots.

My "discussion" with the others began two nights ago in that Dallas hotel, the one Chad scored for us as headquarters. I got no complaints about the place. But it don't give him the right to give orders, a fact that still hasn't registered in that egotistical brain of his.

It had been about 7:00 PM when our cell phones all lit up, all with the same instructions.

Attached find e-ticket for your trip to Iraq the day after tomorrow. Please bring bathing suits.

That's it. No name. No ID. Not that there had to be. We all knew it was from the Watchers, the little group of people, or whatever they are, who've been running us all over the place. Again, no complaints.

Truth is, things were pretty boring 'til they came along. But this assignment, and with Daniel, well, it was way over the top. And as we sat around Chad's living room, I couldn't of made it clearer.

And their response?

"You worry too much," Chad had said, putting away another brew. "Ask me, you're smothering the kid."

"Smothering?" I felt my jaw tighten.

He nodded and belched. "Definitely time to cut the apron strings."

"Cut the apron—"

"If you ask me—"

"No one's asking you, pretty boy. Fact is, you're the last one I'd be asking."

"Which is your whole problem." He motioned to Andi, sitting at the computer, and Cowboy, who sat beside Daniel, who was playing one of them cell phone games. "Before you guys met me, you were nothing—no plans, no organization, just stumbling around in the dark chasing your tails."

"Listen, you arrogant piece of—"

Andi coughed loudly. I glanced to her and swallowed back the words. I been doin' pretty good in the language department; tryin' real hard with Daniel around. But this jerk, he made it so . . . let's just say he knew how to push my vocab buttons. Particularly the blue ones.

"Guys, guys—" Cowboy (aka Tank) raised his meaty hand. As usual he was trying to be the peace maker.

"Not now," I said. "He may have you all fooled, getting this hotel and playin' his mind tricks." I turned back to Chad. "But you and me, we know different, don't we?"

He tried to hold my gaze but knew what I meant—the stuff I saw when we crossed through the portal together, when we entered that snowflake thing and I saw all those ugly pieces of his past life. Yeah, I knew the real Chad Thorton, top to bottom, and he knew I knew.

I continued. "Daniel, he's my responsibility and I'm done putting him in danger."

"Smother, smother, smother."

I swallowed, fighting back the impulse to rearrange his face. I'd done it before and he knew I could do it again.

"Your kid looks in pretty good shape to me," he said.

"And the scar in his back?" I said. "That fairy thing practically killed him."

Andi stepped in, nice and gentle. "But it didn't."

"This time."

Pretty Boy didn't let up. "The kid's got powers and gifts just like the rest of us. Not as developed as mine, no one's is, but the potential's there. And he was the only one who kept his head and didn't freak when we were stuck on that cruise ship trying to figure out who we were."

"He's got a point, Miss Brenda," Cowboy said. "The Watchers put him on the team for some reason."

I motioned to the message on Andi's computer and on our cells. "There ain't no way in heaven or hell I'm letting him go to Iraq."

"Miss Bren—"

"People die over there, Cowboy. Every day."

"People die everywhere," Pretty Boy sighed.

10

"And the professor's words?" Cowboy said. "About Heaven and Earth needing us? And those angels chained under the Euphrates River?"

"Which, I might point out, runs directly through the heart of Iraq," Chad added.

Time to go. I got to my feet. "Be sure to send me selfies."

"Hold it," Chad said. "You're staying behind, too?"

"A boy needs his mother."

That's when everything got real quiet. No one had ever turned down the Watchers before. And now that things were heatin' up . . .

"Maybe," Cowboy cleared his throat. "Maybe we should chew on it for the night. I mean it does sound kinda dangerous."

Chad snickered. "So Bible boy is chickening out, too?"

"I didn't say—"

"You can sleep all you want," I said, "but there ain't no way I'm taking this child to Iraq. Come on, Daniel."

He got up and joined me, eyes still glued to his cell phone.

The plane lurched, pulling me from my thoughts. I focused on the sketchpad. I was drawin' butterflies. I had them flyin' over a cool park with flowers and trees and a stream. Each one had an eye on both of their wings with all sorts of designs around them.

I shook my head over the conversation. It was true, I'd made up my mind about me and Daniel. There was no human way I would change it. Then again, with these little trips, we weren't always talking about human . . .

Chapter 2

The plane hit the runway, rose slightly and hit again, harder. I guess they call that landing. As we taxied toward the terminal my mind again drifted back to how I got here . . .

"Sleeping on it," like Cowboy suggested, didn't exactly go the way I had planned. Or like any of us planned. Turns out the professor had shown up again. Not in a mirror like before, or on a boat, but in my dream. In everyone's dreams. That's what we learned when we all got together that next morning.

Now, 'fore we go any farther, let me make it clear he ain't no ghost. Least we don't think so. To be a ghost you gotta die. And as far as we can tell the professor isn't dead. Just found a way to slip into some higher dimension or alternate universe or whatever the brainiacs call it. Like that village place we visited where Little Foot comes from.

Least that's what we figure.

Back to the dreams. Sitting in the living room the next morning I had been the first to break the ice and tell mine.

"So," I said, "I was in my shop tatting a dancing

couple on some lady's ankle when the couple came alive and began dancing all over her leg. And the man, he looked exactly like the professor."

Everyone got real quiet. Andi turned to her desk computer and typed the word:

Dancing

"What type of dance?" Chad said.

"What difference does it make?"

"A waltz, the twist, some sort of ballroom thing?"

"The polka?" Andi asked.

I looked at her surprised. "Yeah, maybe. How did you know?"

She explained as she typed:

Polka

"Believe it or not, it was his favorite dance."

We traded looks and chuckled. The old dude was full of surprises.

"And Tank?" Andi said. "You dreamed about him, too?"

Cowboy glanced away, a little embarrassed.

"Tank?"

"Yeah." He cleared his throat. "I was back in my college anatomy class."

"You were in college?" Chad asked.

"Football," I said. "Big time scholarship."

"Of course." Chad said. "Nothing that required opening a book."

I ignored him. We all did.

Cowboy continued. "The professor, he was up

front teaching and he'd drawn a picture on the board."

"A picture of what?" Chad asked.

Cowboy glanced down.

Andi repeated the question. "What was the picture of, Tank?"

The big guy finally looked up and swallowed. "You."

I tried not to smile. We all knew Cowboy had a crush on her. Now it sounded like she'd worked her way from his heart into his dreams.

"Your face," he said.

The slightest color rose to her cheeks.

"Anything else?" I asked.

"He had an arrow pointing to your mouth."

She hesitated, then turned and typed:

Mout-

He interrupted. "Actually, it was your lips."

More hesitation. She deleted the word and typed:

Lips

We sat there a moment staring at the words on the screen.

Dancing Polka Lips

I turned to Andi. "What about you?"

She nodded. "I was in the professor's office, only it looked like a doctor's office. He was wearing the obligatory stethoscope and was examining my throat, having me say, 'Ahhh . . .'"

15

I nodded and motioned her to write it down. She turned and typed:

Ahhh . . .

"What about you, Chad?" Cowboy said.
"I got nothing. Just a peaceful night's rest."
Selfish even in his sleep. Why wasn't I surprised?
We turned back to look at the screen.

Dancing Polka Lips Ahhh . . .

"So what are we talking here?" Chad said. "Multi-dimensional charades?"
Studying the screen, Andi answered, "Whatever it was, he was clearly speaking in code."
"Like he didn't want others to know what he was saying," Cowboy said.
"That's why they call it code," Chad said.
We ignored him and kept staring at the words.
"Get rid of the *Dancing* or the *Polka*," he said. "You can't have two of the same thing."
Andi nodded. "We'll lose *Dancing*."
"Because?" I asked.
She lowered her voice, doing her best imitation of the professor, "One must never speak in generalities when one has the opportunity to be specific."
She deleted the word. We kept staring at the screen:

Polka Lips Ahhh . . .

Finally Chad said, "You're kidding me, right?

You don't see it?"

"See what?" Andi asked.

"Really? You're that dense? Flip it around. Put the *Ahhh* . . . first."

Andi cut and pasted for the screen to read:

Ahhh . . . Polka Lips

"I don't get it," Cowboy said.

"Come on people. Look!" Chad sighed. "Ahhh polka lips. Ah-polka-lips."

Andi was the next to get it: "Apocalypse?"

"Couldn't be any clearer," Chad said.

I frowned. "He's telling us the world is coming to an end?"

"You think?"

"Or . . ." Andi said more thoughtfully, "that's what our mission is supposed to be." No one answered, so she explained. "Those four angels he told us about, the ones under the river?" She turned to Cowboy. "They're in the book of Revelation, right?"

"Yes, ma'am, chapter nine."

"And Revelation, that's where the Apocalypse supposedly takes place."

He nodded.

"So . . ."

"We're somehow involved with the Apocalypse?" he asked. "The end of the world?"

I spoke slower, thinking out loud. "And that's what they expect Daniel to risk his life over?"

"Don't think you'll have to worry about that," Chad said.

"What? Why?" I turned to him.

His eyes were closed and his hand raised. "Shhh . . ."

"What are you—"

"Quiet." He scowled like he was concentrating. Everyone traded looks, then he continued, "If you go to his room, you'll find he's long gone."

"He's what?"

Eyes still closed, he spoke like he was repeating someone:

"I'll be okay, Mom. You got to go. Don't stay because of me. Don't look for me, you won't find me."

"Daniel—"

Chad opened one eye. "Will you shut up, please?" After another moment he continued, "I promise I'm safe. I'm hiding so you can't find me. So you can go. You've got to go."

"Dan—"

"They say it's real important. You got to go."

"Daniel, you just can't—"

"I lost him." Chad opened his eyes. "Guess he's done talking."

"What? Where is he?"

"Don't know."

"What do you mean you don't know? Of course you know!"

He shook his head. "He's put up some kind of block. I told you he's talented."

Andi gasped and we all turned to her. On her computer one letter after another began to form. Big letters that filled the whole screen:

GO MOM!

That was thirty-six hours ago. And yes, I'd checked his room. And yes, I looked everywhere I could think of. But if there was anybody more stubborn than me, it was Daniel. And like Pretty Boy said, the kid was smart.

But we weren't done. Not quite. One more e-mail came in. Just last night. Like the first one, it popped up on all our cell phones.

And it was the one that finally got me on this plane:

Daniel is safe.
He is under our protection.
Your participation is vital.
Don't forget those bathing suits.

Chapter 3

Taxiing into the terminal at Bagdad was uneventful. Wish I could say the same about going through Immigration. I get it when they give body searches *before* you get on the plane. But when you get off? Makes no sense. Especially all the extra attention they gave me and Andi. Then again, it might have had something to do with all them guards being male.

That wasn't my only hassle. We'd barely landed before my head began filling up with all sorts of pictures. The type I see when I tat someone's past or future. But this was mostly ugly stuff. Killings, murders, tortures.

First, I figured it had to do with the war. But the clothes were all wrong. Lots of robes, which I suppose could be from today, but somehow they looked different. Way older. A few even had gowns and furs with jewels like kings or somethin'.

Then there were the animals. Some I recognized, like the lions in a pit with some kid. But the others— dragons, creatures full of eyes, spinning wheels full of eyes. But what really got my attention were the winged things with tail stingers. The ones that looked exactly like the fairy that attacked Daniel down in Mexico.

Luckily they started to fade and were completely gone by the time we got to the luggage carousel.

Once we grabbed our backpacks and stepped out of the terminal you could literally taste the dust. And the heat? I'm used to the desert. But 110 in the shade is pushing it even for me.

"Excuse me! Excuse me!" Some skinny, fossil of a man waved a cardboard sign with our names on it. "You are the Americans, yes?"

He seemed kinda familiar but I couldn't put my finger on it. Anyway, we nodded and he broke into a grin, showing a serious lack of dental hygiene. "Bijan Rezaei at your service. I am your driver."

He turned to the old Fiat behind him and pried open the passenger door. I noticed most of the right fender was missing and I couldn't make out the car's color. Hard to tell under all the layers of caked mud and dirt.

"This is your car?" Cowboy asked.

"Yes. Please."

"Figures," I muttered.

I slid into the back seat. Cowboy followed and took the middle, poor guy. But that was only 'cause Chad whined about getting carsick and said he needed the window. Of course he took time to wipe down the seat so he wouldn't get his pretty-boy white pants dirty.

"They're Ralph Lauren," he said. "Two hundred seventy dollars, and that's a steal."

I shook my head. Some things just aren't worth commenting on.

Andi took the front seat and looked for the non-existent seat belt.

"Do we have air conditioning?" Pretty Boy asked.

"Oh, yes, yes. The best. I have only the best."

Which of course meant he had none at all. Unless you count the front passenger window which was broken and couldn't be rolled up. No complaints. It gave a nice breeze as we cruised the city streets . . . but turned to a hurricane when he hit the open road and tried to set a new land speed record.

"How far?" I shouted over the roaring wind.

"Very well, thank you. And you?"

I leaned forward, yelled louder. "No, no. Where are we going? How far is it?"

"Just over 100 kilometers. We will be there very soon."

"No doubt," I muttered, "the way you're driving."

"And where is 'there'?" Andi asked.

"Ramadi. My home town."

The name meant nothing, at least to me. I sat back and closed my eyes. Big mistake. The pictures came back. This time angels with swords. Big fellas, cutting down anything in their path—animals, trees . . . people.

Bijan dropped in a cassette, his version of music—if you call all the yelping and screaming music.

I glanced over to Chad. For the first time in a long time he wasn't talking. A welcome relief. But something felt wrong.

"Hey," I called. "Pretty Boy."

He gave a start and opened his eyes.

"You okay?"

"I'm better than okay. I'm brilliant."

I wasn't surprised by the words. But it was his attitude. Totally missing. And Chad Thorton without attitude meant something was wrong. Still, the joy of his silence was a relief. I didn't want to mess it up with any more questions.

The sun had just started to set when we rolled into the ruins of what the driver called Ramadi.

"Pull over!" Chad yanked at his door. "Pull over!"

"What's wrong?" Cowboy said.

"Pull over!"

The driver barely made it to the side of the road before Pretty Boy tumbled out and hurled his lunch.

"Is he okay?" Andi asked.

"Carsick," I guessed.

"I don't know," Cowboy said. "He looked a little peaked even 'fore we landed."

"I do not think it is carsickness," Bijan said. He shook his head. "No, I do not."

Before we could ask what he meant, Chad climbed back inside.

"Are you okay?" Andi asked.

"Of course," he said as he adjusted his pants and made sure the car seat was still clean. "Just a little carsickness."

I glanced to the rearview mirror. Bijan was shaking his head as he pulled back into traffic.

Ramadi was a war zone. Literally. A rusting, leftover tank lay on one side of the road. Two gutted and overturned armored trucks sat on the other. Not far away a third rested on its axels, its tires long gone. Collapsed concrete buildings were everywhere.

Dozens of stories stacked right on top of each other like so many pancakes.

"Were you here during the war?" Andi asked Bijan.

"Yes, yes," he said. "It was very bad."

"And your family?" Cowboy asked.

He didn't answer.

Cowboy spoke louder. "Do you have family here?"

He shook his head. "They have left. My wife, my boys, they are gone."

"To some place safe?" I said. "Away from the fighting?"

"Yes, very far away. And they are happy. Heaven, it is a very happy place."

We traded looks.

"Heaven?" Andi repeated.

"Yes, they are in Heaven. Very safe. Very happy."

"I'm sorry," Andi said more softly.

"They are very happy."

We didn't know what to say. We didn't have to.

He continued. "Because my wife, because she became Christian they wanted me to stone her. That is the penalty for conversion. When I refused, they drove me out to the desert, many, many kilometers and made me walk home. Three days and two nights."

"That's terrible," Andi said.

"I was the lucky one. My wife, my children, not so much."

"Because ISIS was here, because they invaded the city?" she asked.

"No. They made it worse, yes. Very much

worse."

"But you," Andi gently persisted, "you survived."

He motioned across the wide, river we'd been following "Just over there. I was in prison so I was safe."

"You were safe?" I repeated. "In prison?"

"Not from the devils, but from everything else."

"Devils," I said. "You mean the guards?"

"No, no. The devils. The four devils who will become loosed unless you do something. That is why you are here. Yes?"

We had no idea how to answer.

He looked in the mirror. "Perhaps . . ." He hesitated. "Before I take you to your hotel, perhaps I should show you."

Before we could answer, he threw the car into a U-turn. Horns honked, tires squealed. No one was happy, least of all Bijan's passengers. But somehow we avoided getting killed.

I hoped our luck would continue.

Chapter 4

Minutes later we were on a narrow road crossing the river. But it wasn't a bridge.

"Are we on top of a dam?" Andi asked.

"Yes, a dam. You are correct."

"And the river, it's the Euphrates?"

"You are in the cradle of civilization. The Garden of Eden was here in my country. And the tower of Babel."

"And Abraham," Cowboy chimed in. "Isn't this where he started out?"

"And Nebuchadnezzar and Daniel. And buried here we have the bones of Ezekiel, Ezra and Jonah."

"That's a lot of Bible," Cowboy said.

"Iraq, it means *country of deep roots*. Next to Israel, there is no country mentioned more in the Bible."

But I wasn't as interested in history as in what I saw. "This dam," I said, "everything about it—the road, the walls—everything's in perfect condition."

"Yes," Bijan said.

"But everything else in the city is ruined—

26

buildings, homes. Why wasn't the dam destroyed?"

"Which is the reason you are here."

"Come again?"

"There are many cities downstream of this river. Using the dam, ISIS cut off all their water. When we won back the city and reopened the floodgates, it changed the river's course slightly."

"What's that got to do with us?" I said.

"And the four devils who will be loosed?" Andi asked.

We'd reached the end of the dam. Instead of answering, Bijan turned right onto a road even worse than the last one. "Just ahead, you see those buildings?"

I craned my neck and spotted a big, broken down complex. Most of the roof was gone. Walls were collapsed and crumbling. And rubble. Everywhere you looked, rubble.

"This is where I was in prison. On the banks of this river."

He slowed the car. I heard a moan and saw Chad holding his head. He looked pretty bad.

But Bijan continued. "This is where we heard the screams. Every day. Every night. As the river dried they grew louder and louder. Many of my fellow inmates, I am sorry to say, their minds, they have not been the same."

"They went crazy?" Cowboy asked.

"Yes."

"From the screams?"

"It is difficult to explain. They were more than screams. We felt them inside. Our heads, our souls. They never stopped."

"Where did they come from?" Andi asked.

"Below. The prison, it was built upon a large cavern. The only entrance to the cavern and the only exit was through a cave far underneath the river."

"And then the river changed course."

"Yes. Not much. But our neighbor to the north, Turkey, she is hoarding water and now the level drops every day."

"Time out," I said. "You're telling us these devils are somehow trapped in a cavern sealed up by water?"

"Yes. But as the course changes, as the water level lowers, they are much closer to escaping."

Silence stole over the car . . . until Cowboy recited the verses from Revelation, the ones the professor had given us:

"And I heard a voice saying . . . Loose the four angels which are bound in the great river Euphrates. And the four angels were loosed, which were prepared to slay the third part of men."

More silence. I took a breath, then asked the question we'd all been thinking. "And what exactly do you want from us? Why are we here?"

Bijan looked in the mirror, cocked his head. "I thought I said."

"Remind me again."

"To prevent their escape."

"'They' being . . ."

"The angels, the devils."

I blinked and swore. I figured Andi and Cowboy were doing the same but in a more PG version.

And Chad?

"Stop the car!" he shouted. "Stop!"

Bijan pulled over, but this time he was too late. Pretty boy choked up the last of his meal . . . all over those pricey Ralph Laurens.

"Say, Bijan?" Cowboy said.

"Yes?"

"Now might be a good time to visit our hotel."

"Yes, I agree. Your equipment, it is already in place so tomorrow you can get an early start."

We traded looks. But he wasn't done.

"And bathing suits? I believe you were instructed to bring bathing suits?"

"For what?" I said.

"To enter the cavern."

"What are you talking about?"

"To ensure the angels remain bound there is no other way."

Chapter 5

One thing you can say about the Watchers, they treat us good. The hotel was top notch. Well, as top notch as you could get in Ramadi. (Think of a two-star Motel 6 with cockroaches the size of Volkswagens).

Still, no major complaints. Least the place had showers. Okay, one. And who needed hot water in all that afternoon heat?

Anyways, the sun had just set and I'd barely toweled off and thrown on some clothes before the boys came into our room.

Chad still wasn't doing well.

"You look like crap," I said.

"I look better than I feel."

"It's the voices," Cowboy said.

"Voices?"

"Yeah."

Chad crossed to the sofa and was ready to sit.

"Might want to check under that cushion first," I said.

He bent down and flipped it over. Good call. A

dozen silverfish scurried for shelter.

"By voices, you mean impressions?" Andi asked.

He plopped down and nodded.

"But you get those all the time. That's one of your gifts."

"Not like these, I don't. These mothers are mean. Vicious."

"Demons," Cowboy corrected.

I arched a brow.

Chad answered. "Me and Jock-o here, we've been talking. He says if I'm not careful, my gift can turn on me."

"Meaning?"

Cowboy answered, "The spirit world has a good side, but it also has a dark side. Our gifts are kinda like doorways."

I walked to the window and looked out into the night. It sounded like we were in for another sermon. I wasn't wrong.

"If we don't ask God to stand guard, the bad spirits can come in and really mess things up."

"Demons," Andi repeated.

"That's right. But Jesus, he has authority over them."

I turned to Cowboy. "This from a guy whose faith nearly crumbled when we ran into that fairy thing?"

He smiled. "He's also pretty forgiving."

I looked back out the window.

Chad motioned to Cowboy. "So the troll here, he's been telling me I have to give my gifts to God or I'll always be open to—" he made air quotes— "deception."

Cowboy nodded. "Occult counterfeit."

No one answered. Without turning from the window, I said, "I suppose that goes for me, too? And Daniel?"

"It goes for all of us, Miss Brenda. Look, I don't mind praying for everyone's protection, but it'd sure be easier if you'd ask the Lord for yourselves."

I looked to Andi, our resident Jew. She didn't seem bothered. Either she was cutting Cowboy slack or, like me, she was starting to buy into all his superstitious mumbo-jumbo. A year ago I would have chewed him up and spit him out.

But that was a year ago.

I looked back into the night just in time to see a blazing something fill the sky. It was big and getting bigger by the second. I blinked hard and it was gone. Another vision. I swore under my breath.

"So," Andi said, changing the subject. "Who here has ever gone spelunking?"

"Spe— what?" Cowboy asked.

"Cave exploring," Chad said.

I turned to her. "You're serious about doing that?"

"The Watchers certainly are serious."

"Is it just me, or is each assignment getting weirder?" I asked.

"It's just a cave," Chad said, obviously trying to regain his macho status.

"He's right," Andi said.

"Right," I said. "And tell me again, what exactly are they using to lock up angels these days?"

Quiet chuckles all around . . . 'cept for Cowboy.

I continued. "And another thing. If God's supposed to be, you know, all God-like, and he says it's time to let the angels go, then who are we to—"

"He doesn't," Cowboy said.

"Come again?"

"The timing, it's wrong. The angels, they're not supposed to be released 'til other things happen first."

"Other things? Like what?"

He shook his head. "Ugly things."

"So they're trying to jump the gun?"

Cowboy gave a slow nod. "According to the Bible."

Andi sighed. "Bijan certainly seems to know what he's talking about."

Cowboy agreed. "And he's already brought in the equipment."

"Equipment for what?" I said.

"Dudes," Chad said, straightening.

Andi went on talking. "That would have been a good question to ask him."

"Along with a thousand others."

"Dudes," Chad repeated, "it's Daniel."

I spun to him. His eyes were closed and he was obviously concentrating.

"I thought you were blocked," Cowboy said.

Chad frowned. "Shhh . . ."

We got quiet and waited. Finally, Chad started to quote what he was hearing:

"Having lots of fun."

"Where," I said. "Where is he?"

"Shh."

I bit my tongue and waited.

"I hope you are, too."

"We are what?" Cowboy asked.

"Having fun," Andi said.

Chad continued. "I'm at home, everything is fine. Don't be scared. The Watchers are looking out for me. They're with you, too."

I glanced around the room, half-way expecting to see someone or something in a corner.

"You gotta trust them. Use your gifts like they've trained you."

"Trained?" I asked.

"Will you shut up?" Chad said.

It killed me, but I obeyed.

"Keep having fun."

Chad leaned forward, scowling harder . . . until he sighed and opened his eyes. "That's it. I lost him."

"Lost him?" I said.

"I got blocked."

"But he's okay," Cowboy said, trying to assure me. "He said he was having fun and he's okay."

"That's all you heard?" I asked Chad.

He nodded. "'Til the voices came back."

"The ones you and me have been asking Jesus to stop?" Cowboy said.

Chad glanced around like he was embarrassed, then slowly nodded.

Cowboy smiled. "Don't worry, partner, we'll keep at it. You and me, we'll keep praying."

Chad's face only got redder.

Another round of silence until Andi spoke up. "So . . . we have our assignment. We have our guide."

"And we know the Watchers will be helping," Cowboy said.

"If they're to be trusted," I said.

Andi turned to me. "They've never lied to us before."

It's true. We'd been through a lot. Most of it I don't get. But one thing you can say, they'd never let us down.

"So . . ." Andi looked over the group. "Is everyone in?"

Cowboy nodded.

So did I.

And Pretty Boy? He took a deep breath, paused, and also joined in.

Chapter 6

Next morning we had something the hotel advertised as "A Delightful Continental Buffet to Begin Your Day."

Translation: Bread, cucumbers, bread, tomatoes, bread, goat cheese, bread, and some orange water they called 'orange juice' to help wash down the bread.

"Kind of miss the sausage gravy and biscuits, hey, Jock-o?" Chad asked.

Cowboy grinned. "Yeah."

"Maybe they got some in back. You should go ask."

Cowboy gave him a look and Chad nodded. "Wouldn't hurt."

Taking his cue, Cowboy nodded and rose.

"Tank?" Andi called.

"Maybe they can round up some bacon while they're at it," Chad said. "Oh, and honey-baked ham, now that would be sweet."

"Tank?"

"Yeah, Andi?"

"We're in a Muslim country."

He frowned.

"They don't eat pork."

Cowboy hesitated and looked at Chad, who smirked. The big guy turned and lumbered back to his seat.

"You seem better," I said to Chad.

He nodded to Cowboy. "Trying out the troll's prescription."

"About God?"

He grunted.

"Might be a couple other things to pick up in that department," I said.

"Maybe, but the way I figure, he's got it all wrong."

"Why am I not surprised?"

"No, listen. There's not one doorway. There are two."

"What," I said, "the good one and the bad one?"

"It's a lot more complicated than that. But for your simple mind, yeah, that's close enough."

I was already regretting Cowboy helping Chad feel better. Even more so as we headed up to our rooms to get ready and Chad called, "And don't forget those swim suits. Seeing Andi in a bikini is the only reason I came."

(I'm guessin' some changes take a lot of prayer).

Thirty minutes later we were crammed back into Bijan's car. After crossing the dam and hitting every rut and pothole along the way, we finally arrived at the prison.

It seemed a lot bigger when you were right next

to it. Creepier, too.

"Come," Bijan said. "We have much to do." He grabbed a flashlight from the car and we started out.

Everywhere we looked there were fallen and half-destroyed walls. And it was completely gutted. No furniture. No iron bars. Even the electrical wiring was gone. Just one crumbling passageway after another as Bijan's flashlight played over the empty niches that had once been prison cells.

"How many did this place hold?" Cowboy asked.

"It was designed for 155 people. Before we were liberated there were nearly 1300."

"That's terrible," Andi said.

"Yes, at times it was not so easy."

We entered a narrow stairway, partially hidden. Its walls and descending steps were carved out of stone. It went down forever.

A minute or two later, Chad let out a cry and doubled over.

"You okay, partner?" Cowboy asked.

"Yeah. It's just . . ." He hesitated.

"The voices?" Cowboy said. "They're back?"

Chad took a breath then quietly answered, "Yeah."

Cowboy raised a big paw and set it on the man's shoulder. Without a word he began moving his lips. Ten, twenty seconds later, Pretty Boy looked up and nodded. Cowboy nodded back. And we continued.

Eventually we reached the bottom of the stairway and traveled through another passageway. Fifty yards later we reached the water's edge. It was black and silent. Bijan swept his light across the water to the far wall. It was twenty feet away. The place was no more than ten feet wide. The ceiling was about that high, too.

"And there is your equipment." He directed his light back to our side and the left where we saw a small pile of—

"Diving masks?" Andi asked.

"Yes."

"That's our equipment?" Chad said. "That's all we have?"

"That is all you need. And, of course, your special talents." He motioned to a small niche over to the right. "Ladies, you may change over there. And gentlemen," he swept his light to the left, "over there."

Chad was the last to join us from his changing room.

"You're kidding," I said. "Speedos? Really?"

He flexed his abs which, like it or not, were impressive. "When you got it, flaunt it," he said (which changed their status from impressive to disgusting).

Cowboy was more modest. Like me and Andi, he had gone for the cutoffs and baggy-tee-shirt look.

"Please, you will join me?" Bijan said. He stood waist deep in the water, next to the left wall. His flashlight was the only thing that lit the place.

Cowboy was the first to step in. Not to be outdone, Chad followed. Then Andi. Then me.

"If you reach under the water to your left," Bijan said, "you will feel a rope along the side of this wall. It is threaded through fasteners attached to the stone. It will lead you to your destination."

"Which is . . .?" I asked.

He flashed his beam across the water to the far wall. "It is forty feet beyond that."

"Beyond it?" Cowboy asked.

"Yes."

"But . . . that's a wall."

"And you are going under it."

Andi frowned. "For forty feet?"

"Not to worry. There are many small pockets of air. You will not have to hold your breath the entire way."

"By *small* you mean . . ."

"Six, in some places, ten inches high, now that the river has lowered. And that is our concern. As the river drops the angels will eventually be able to escape."

I frowned. "What, they're allergic to water?"

"This I do not know."

"I'm melting, I'm melting." Chad did his best Wicked Witch of the West impression. We did our best to ignore him.

"Now," Bijan said as he eased deeper into the water, "here you will feel the rope." He motioned for us to follow. We moved forward until the water was up to our chests as we groped along the wall searching for the rope.

"Got it," Chad said.

"Me, too," Andi said.

"And me," Cowboy said.

When I found it, it felt more like a cord than a rope. And slimy, probably from the water.

"You will be in total darkness," Bijan said. "This is your lifeline. "It will take you to air pockets where you must breathe. At no time must you release it. If you do, you will be lost and you will surely . . ." He came to a stop, probably by the looks on our faces. He forced a smile and simply repeated, "It is best not to release the rope."

We nodded like obedient children. Very nervous obedient children.

"Now if everyone is ready, please put on your equipment and follow me." He slipped his mask over his face, then took several deep breaths, turned and disappeared into the black water.

Chapter 7

Chad followed Bijan, Andi followed Chad, then me,
and finally Tank.

If the river was dark on the surface, it was pitch
black underneath. A small part of me wanted to turn
tail and run. Alright, a big part of me. I'm not
claustrophobic, just not a fan of drowning. Dying's
not high on my list, either.

And the cord? At first I cheated. Instead of
following it as it rose back up every ten to fifteen feet
into an air pocket, I tried keeping my head at the
surface all the time.

Only problem was there *was* no surface. Just
rock. Luckily, the water had worn the stone smooth
so there was nothing jagged to cut my head when I
slammed into it. But I was sure getting a mother of a
headache. So I eventually decided to play by the rules.

And just as Bijan said, every time I thought I
needed a breath, the cord led me up to a pocket of

air. I'd hang there a few seconds, take a couple deep breaths, then drop back under. True, the pockets were just as black as the water, but they were a lot easier to breathe.

Unfortunately, all that darkness didn't help with the images in my brain. They came almost immediately and there was nothing I could do to stop them. At first they were innocent enough. Candlesticks, lambs, crowds of people in white robes.

Then things got weird.

A woman, a hooker really, riding some crazy four-footed monster while she's gulping blood from a bowl. She looked directly into my eyes and snarled— red teeth dripping blood that spilled from her mouth and ran down her neck.

Then there was a leopard, but with giant bear paws. And heads. A half dozen of 'em, maybe more. Each one howling and cussing. When they spotted me, their eyes turned into fire with hate so hot I literally felt its heat against my face.

I've seen a lot in my life and ain't no chicken, but this definitely kicked up my pulse. And my need for air. I began to panic. I'd only been under a few seconds, but I needed to breathe. I pulled along the line faster. Little sparkles of light began popping up in my vision. My heart pounded in my ears. And my lungs burned hotter and hotter. I had to put out the fire, suck in the cool, soothing water. Then, true to form, the line suddenly shot up and I was in a pocket of air gulping it down like a mad woman.

The leopard disappeared. I stayed in that pocket, gasping, trying to calm myself. It was just as dark, but at least I was safe . . . until the fairies showed up. Like in Mexico. They darted and dived around my head, coming closer and closer, until one grabbed my hair with its spindly little hands and began yanking. Others joined in, a couple clawing and biting my scalp. Another vision? No doubt. But real enough. With nowhere to go, I took another breath and dropped back under the water.

The cord went deeper than before. And new images appeared. Even more vivid. First there was the sound of hoof beats behind me. They quickly grew into a roar. When I turned, I saw hundreds upon hundreds of horses—black, white, red. And their riders. Some alive, others rotting skeletons.

And blood. Everywhere. And rising. To my knees, waist, chest. The horses were swimming in it, kicking, trying not to drown. My heart hammered in my chest. I had to breathe again. Desperately. But the cord kept going downward.

A dragon came into sight and filled my vision. Red and huge with a tail so big that it literally knocked stars out of the sky. Like the leopard, the dragon had lots of heads. Only with horns. It hissed and lunged at me. But it wasn't me. Well, it was, but it wasn't. One minute I was black, then white, then Asian, then Latin. And pregnant. Every version of me was pregnant.

The first contraction hit hard. So hard I gasped, nearly sucking in the surrounding water. The heads continued to approach, their long necks wrapping around me. One floated just inches from my face, snapping and snarling.

I clenched my jaws, pursed my lips, trying not to suck in the water. But my lungs were on fire again. Screaming and burning for air.

The head nearest my ear had a horn with a

mouth that began screaming vile, obscene things. Suddenly I had to push. It was like I was giving birth. I couldn't stop. Pain seared through my gut. One of the heads dropped onto my belly, its teeth gnashing like it was starving, waiting for my baby to appear so it could eat it. Another was twisting and squirming its way up my legs.

It was too much. The sparkling lights returned. Brighter, bigger. The edges of my vision grew white. My lungs burned, screaming for air. But the baby was coming. I had to stay awake.

I felt the head's tongue, the one on my belly, flicking back and forth in anticipation. The other had slithered up to my knees.

I had to surface.

I let go of the cord and shot up until I slammed into the rock ceiling. Dazed, barely conscious, I worked my hands across the stone, desperate to find an opening.

Nothing.

My heart roared in my ears. I was in full- blown panic. The head moved down my belly, the other up my thigh, shrieking in anticipation. I kicked. I thrashed, groping at the ceiling. I pounded my fists against the rock. Heard a baby scream. Mine? I couldn't tell. Something grabbed me from behind. I fought, I twisted, I kicked. I had no idea where I was, no up or down, as everything grew white, whiter, all white . . . as the sound faded.

And then there was nothing.

I woke up swinging. Didn't know where I was. Didn't matter.

"Easy, Miss Brenda, easy."

I felt Cowboy's big paws holding me down. My head exploded in pain. I would have fought harder, but I had nothing left.

"Easy."

I relaxed. A little. I dropped my head back down onto what felt like grass.

"Pretty impressive," Chad said.

"Well done, Tank," Andi added.

I finally pried open my eyes.

"Welcome back," Chad said.

I focused and saw them staring at me from around a small campfire. Except for Cowboy. He was leaning back on his haunches smiling down at me. The light around us was soft and pinkish like just before sunset. I heard a stream bubbling nearby. And Birds. Lots of chirping and singing.

"What . . ." I swallowed and tried again. "What

happened?

"Not much," Chad said. "Well, except for the part of you drowning and the troll here, bringing you back to life."

"What?"

"Just a little mouth-to-mouth." Chad said. Winking at Cowboy, he added, "Which I'm betting you didn't mind, eh, big guy?"

Cowboy glanced away, obviously embarrassed.

It took some effort, but I finally managed to sit up. That's when I spotted the fawn. She stood beside Andi, nuzzling her arm. "Where are we?"

Chad nodded to Bijan. "Our man here calls it Eden."

"Eden?"

He kicked a bunny sniffing at his shoe. "Scram."

"Eden?" I repeated. "As in . . ."

"The Garden of Eden," Andi said.

I frowned.

"Yeah, I didn't buy it either," Chad said. He nodded towards Andi, "'Til Miss hot and lovely here reminded us."

Ignoring him, she asked me, "Are you sure you're okay? You had us all pretty worried."

"What's he talking about?" I said.

She took a deep breath. "According to the book of Genesis, the Garden of Eden was located between the Tigris and Euphrates rivers."

Cowboy finally spoke. "Which is where we are."

"The general vicinity," she said.

"But that's a myth," I said. "I mean, my grandpa used to preach it, but—"

"Your grandfather was a preacher?" Cowboy interrupted.

"And Grandma the choir director, but the point is—"

"Wow."

"The point is it's a fable, an old wives' tale. It can't be real."

"Then it's doing a pretty good imitation of it," Chad said, gesturing at our surroundings.

"I was certainly surprised," Andi said. "For numerous reasons. Not the least of which is the complete lack of archeological evidence."

Bijan spoke up. "Yes, it is, how do you put it, 'well hidden.'"

I looked at the campfire. Not that we needed it, the light and temperature were perfect. But it was a nice effect. It would have been nicer if something was actually burning. Instead the flames came from a small hole with rocks set around it so it looked like a campfire.

"Where's the wood?" I said.

Bijan chuckled. "Oh my, no. Nothing ever dies here. And nothing is ever allowed to be destroyed."

"And the fire?"

"Comes from a thermal vent. There are several such fires scattered around the garden, here." He motioned up to the sky . . . which was actually rock, fifty or so feet above our heads. "The entire garden, it is lit by the vent's reflection, and heated to this perfect temperature."

A butterfly drifted close to my face and I waved it away. "So you knew this was here all along?"

"Yes."

"But . . . the voices? You said you and the other prisoners heard—"

"I am sorry to say that was a lie." He nodded to

Chad. "As were the voices in his head. And the many ugly images you saw as we were diving."

He knew what I had seen? I shook my head. "I don't understand."

"Security," Andi said.

"They were guards," he said. "Barriers to stop the curious and persistent."

"Wait a minute," I said. "Nobody can get inside my head without my permission."

"Unless you count the force field around the Psychic Institute where we first met," Andi said.

Cowboy added, "Or what happened to Andi in Florida."

"Or on our little boat trip,'" Chad said.

"Or the house in that Italian cliff," Cowboy added. "The one that wasn't there."

"Actually, it was there," Bijan said. "It simply appeared from another universe."

"Wait a minute," Cowboy said. "You knew about that?"

"Your adventures, all of them I have watched. We have watched them all."

"We?" Cowboy said.

"Watched?" I repeated.

He looked at me, unable to hold back a grin.

"Watched?" I said again. "As in 'Watchers?' You're one of them, one of the Watchers?"

He chuckled. "A far cry, I am afraid. No, Signora. I am, only, how do you say, a worker bee."

"Signora," Andi said. "That's Italian."

"Si."

"But you're from Iraq," Cowboy said.

Bijan turned to the big guy and grinned.

I frowned, trying to think, but the pounding in

my head made it pretty hard. Still, bits and pieces floated together. "We've met," I said. "There was something familiar about you at the airport."

"Yes. I not only drive cab for you in Iraq. I drive for you once before. Where fish, they fell from the heavens. Where they rained down upon us like—"

"Rome!" Cowboy exclaimed. "You were our cab driver in Rome!"

He nodded. "At your service."

"So what are you doing here?" I asked.

"What are *we* doing here?" Andi said.

"Your world is about to become very, very dark, very, very soon."

"And you guys need our help," Chad said.

"We've been helping you for months," I said.

He answered. "Yes and no. For months the Watchers have been testing you. Giving you little assignments."

"Little?" I scoffed. "They nearly got us killed. More than once."

"Yes. Still, they thought it important for your skills to test, your gifts to observe. And equally important, to see how you cooperate with one another."

I threw a look to Chad.

"And now?" Cowboy asked.

"And now we have little time to waste."

"Time to . . ."

"Unspeakable things are about to occur. You each have a remarkable gift. If you are willing, now is the time to let us help you focus them. To bring them to their fullest potential for the upcoming conflict."

No one spoke. There was only the brook, the birds, and flickering fire.

Finally Cowboy ventured, "By conflict, are you saying, do you mean something like . . . the Apocalypse?"

Bijan's voice was soft but steady as he held Cowboy's gaze. "Yes my friend, that is exactly what I mean."

Chapter 9

Back to the garden, or whatever it was. Definitely impressive. Lush green grass, trimmed trees, manicured bushes . . . and flowers, lots of them. Some I'd never seen before. And the animals. Seriously, I felt like Snow White or whoever that Disney chick was with all the animals hangin' around her. Near Cowboy was something that must have been a llama. Then there was that family of raccoons. Even a panther, kinda shy, was slinking around us.

Bijan told us to spread out, go someplace by ourselves and practice.

"Practice what?" Cowboy asked.

"Why, your gifts, of course."

"How?"

"And where?" Andi said.

"Just begin walking. The right place you will find soon enough."

I motioned to a tall wall off in the distance. Looked like it went all the way to the ceiling. "What's that?"

"In the ancient language, the word *paradise*, it means *walled garden*."

I glanced around. Saw his point.

"You didn't answer the troll," Chad said. "These gifts, how are we supposed to practice them?"

"In your world there is much noise. It is difficult to discover your gift, much less nurture it. Here there is nothing but stillness. As you let it settle your soul, your gift, it will surface and grow."

"So they'll get stronger?" Cowboy asked. "So we can fight the darkness?"

"Yes."

"The darkness that's coming soon," I said.

"Yes, yes. But you must hurry. There is little time."

We stood a moment looking at each other.

"Go," he said, "please go, go. One hour is all I ask. I will wait right here for your return."

Yeah, we had more than a few unanswered questions. But the guy was obviously sincere and it sure seemed pretty important to him. Besides, the place was peaceful enough. If things worked and we got stronger, great. If not, no biggie. What would it hurt?

I was the first to leave. With a shrug, I turned and started down one of the paths. "Catch you in an hour," I said.

The others agreed.

After a couple minutes I found a grassy spot beside a still, quiet pool. Talk about peaceful. Well, except for that grizzly. He sort of crept up on me. When I finally spotted him he was a dozen feet away. I froze. I doubted I breathed. But he just kept coming—eight feet, five feet, three, until he was right beside me. He lowered his big head and pressed his muzzle into my shoulder. I waited. He gave a long, loud sniff. My heart pounded in my throat. He sniffed again—then gave a sudden, disgusted snort before turning and sauntering off.

I took a couple breaths to shake it off. Then a couple more. When my heart finally dropped back down into my chest, I turned back to the pool. Now it was just me, the pool, and a butterfly that occasionally flitted past. It was beautiful, just like the ones I'd sketched on the plane. Complete with a black circle that looked like an eye on each wing.

Pretty soon, as I kept staring at the pool, I began seeing stuff. Vague at first, but the visions got clearer and clearer.

First, I saw soldiers. They wore old fashioned clothes and helmets, like from five hundred years ago. And there were priests beside them in long robes. And people with dunce hats.

That's when I heard the screaming. From the people. And for a pretty good reason. One was having boiling water poured over his naked body. Another was having his tongue cut out. Another had hot coals they were putting on his eyes.

As I kept staring, the images rose out of the water. Kinda like a 3-D movie. And the sounds got clearer. Over the screaming I heard the priests shouting orders. Sounded like they were in Spanish.

Things were getting pretty gruesome so I tried forcing the images to go away. Unlike being in the underwater tunnel, they did. They dissolved to mist and fell back into the pool.

But others followed. Knights on horseback. With

swords and lances they hacked down foot soldiers left and right. Others were on the ground fighting hand to hand. This time they were shouting in English. And there was blood. Everywhere. On their swords, their suits of armor, their shields. Shields, by the way, that had crosses on them. And lions. And dragons. But mostly crosses.

One knight was raising his sword over a guy on the ground and shouting, "To the glory of King Richard and our Lord Jesus Christ!" I forced the image away, but not before I heard the sound of breaking bone and cartilage, followed by a dull thud of what had to be the guy's head falling onto the mud.

Another picture followed. This one at night. A shouting mob circled a young woman who was being burned at the stake. She writhed and screamed—the flames from her clothes already covering her face—as the mob kept shouting, "Confess! Confess! Confess!"

I'd had enough. I stopped the vision. I turned from the pool and rose to my feet . . . just a little unsteady. I don't know how long I'd been there, but I'd seen enough.

"You saw the Inquisition," Chad said.

"The what?"

He turned from me to Andi. "Am I right, sweet cheeks?"

Less than an hour had passed and we'd all returned and were giving our reports.

Andi answered. "Priests." She turned to me. "It sounds like you were seeing priests. And the type of tortures you mentioned, the dunce hats, the style of clothing—"

"Not to mention they spoke Spanish," Chad said. "What else could she have seen but the Spanish

Inquisition? Lot of people died back then."

Andi nodded. "At least thirty thousand."

Chad whistled.

"And them knights?" Cowboy asked. "With their swords and crosses on their shields?"

"It sounds like the Crusades," she said. "'To the glory of King Richard and Jesus Christ.' That was one of their battle cries."

"How many died there?" I asked.

"There are different estimates, but all totaled and conservatively . . ." She took a deep breath and continued, "One and a half million, total."

"And that woman burned at the stake?" I asked. "Was she like a witch?"

"Most likely." Andi continued, "Between the years 1450 and 1750 roughly fifty thousand were burned at the stake in Europe and America."

Chad scoffed and shook his head. "Religion at its finest."

I glanced over to Cowboy. He wasn't amused. Who could blame him? Not a great track record however you looked at it. I turned back to Andi. "What about you? What did you get out there?"

"With your thing for patterns," Chad added.

She hesitated. Took another breath and said, "You've all heard of the Bible Code?"

"Educate me," I said.

She explained. "When you write out the Torah, the first five books of the Bible, in the original Hebrew, and when you align the letters into various columns . . . well, certain patterns appear. Patterns that some scholars believe to be prophetic warnings."

"Such as?" I said.

"Such as spelling out and connecting the word

'Hitler' with 'Nazi.' Or the Kennedy assassination with 'Dallas.'" She hesitated, then added, "Or 'assassination' with the name of the murdered Israeli Prime Minister, 'Yitzhak Rabin.'"

"All that from the holy word of God?" Cowboy asked.

She nodded.

"And . . .?" I said, waiting for more.

"I followed one of the paths to the wall. Carved in the rock were several pages of Hebrew. I recognized they were from the book of Genesis." She looked down.

"Go on," Chad said.

"The words had been stacked, arranged in patterns that I had never seen before.

"And . . ."

"And each time the name for 'God' or 'Lord' appeared . . . it was directly associated with one of three words." She took another breath. It was clear she didn't want to go on, but Chad kept pushing.

"And they were?"

She closed her eyes then softly said the words: "Tyrant. Oppressor. Dictator."

Chapter 10

Silence stole over the group. Cowboy was definitely not happy.

Chad couldn't care less. "And don't forget yours truly," he said.

We turned to him, waiting for his report.

He began. "It's like the stiller I got, the better I got. Without all the distractions my powers really kicked butt."

"To read minds?" I said.

"Yeah, and not just some loser from the mindless masses. I got some real clear stuff from some majorly important dudes."

"Like who?" I said.

He paused then with dramatic flair said, "I, Chad Thorton, got to read the Pope's mind."

"The Pope?" Cowboy said. "As in Rome?"

"I told you I'm good. And not just the Pope, I also read some of the top preacher guys you see on TV. And, for the grand finale, I slipped back into time and even got into the head of Mother Teresa."

"Mother Teresa," Andi asked. "The great humanitarian?"

"Yeah, only not so great. The stuff she was thinking? Whew. Ugly. Racist. Intolerant. Lots of hatred inside that chick."

"No way," Cowboy said.

"Oh yeah, 'big way.' And the same thing with the Pope. I'm serious. And don't even get me started on those TV guys. The bigger they were, the badder they thought."

"I don't . . ." Cowboy scowled. "That can't be true."

Chad shook his head. "No offense, troll man, but your team . . . let's just say they're not the good guys they pretend to be. Fact is, it's just the opposite. From what I saw your heroes are just following in the footsteps of their boss."

"What does that mean?" I said.

"Every one of them is being manipulated by the biggest bad dude of all, the man upstairs."

"Hold it," Andi said, "wait just a minute."

"You said it yourself, sweet cheeks. It's right there in the holy book: Tyrant. Oppressor. Dictator."

"You're certainly not implying—"

"And you, ghetto girl." He nodded to me. "When it comes to the big dude's history, he doesn't exactly have the cleanest slate, does he?"

Things got quiet again. Real quiet. We just sat there, trying to wrap our heads around what we'd heard. Yeah, I get that Chad wasn't known for his understatements or his humility. But if half of what he said was true . . . or what I saw . . . or what Andi read—I mean, if God really was some sort of tyrant and dictator. . .

I turned back to Cowboy. His face was more than a little red. No surprise. I mean if he and God were such pals and his pal turned out to be a bad guy . . .

Andi saw his struggle, too. And asked quietly, "What about you, Tank?"

He stared into the campfire. "What about me?"

"Your gifts. Did they get any stronger? What did you experience?"

"I—" he stopped.

We traded looks.

"You what?" Chad said.

"I got . . ." He shook his head and softly admitted, "I got nothing."

"Nothing?"

He kept quiet.

Chad pushed. "Nothing at all?"

He shook his head.

Chad sat back and gave another low whistle.

I turned to him. "What does that mean?"

"You tell me," he said. "Here we are in Paradise. All of our gifts are amping up and Bible boy is getting nothing?" He folded his hands behind his head "Maybe Jocko here has been playing for the wrong team. Maybe his boss is the one who's the monster— the megalomaniac the one who tortures and—"

Cowboy leaped to his feet and grabbed Chad's throat. "Take it back!" he roared. "Take it back!"

"Tank!" Andi shouted.

Chad kicked and twisted trying to get free. But Cowboy squeezed tighter. "Take it back!"

"Cowboy!"

"Take it back now!"

THROUGH A GLASS DARKLY

"Tank!" I yelled.

Chad's eyes bulged. His face turned crimson.

"Tank!" Andi raced to them, yanked at Cowboy's arm. "He can't breathe!"

But his grip was a vice. Chad squirmed, tried, but could not pry away Cowboy's hands.

Andi got right into the big man's face. "Tank! Tank! You're killing him!"

His eyes shifted to hers.

"Tank!"

He tried looking away from her, but he couldn't.

"Let go of him," she said. "This is not what God wants. Tank . . ."

He kept staring at her. She nodded, spoke softly, evenly. "Let him go."

He blinked.

She held his gaze. Nodded again, slower.

Finally, reluctantly, Tank released Chad.

Pretty Boy dropped to the ground, coughing and gasping for air.

And Bijan, who had been quiet until now, finally spoke. "And that, my friends, is why you are here." We turned to him as he reached out his hands. "Join us. Help us break the chains. Free your planet from the tyrannical hold."

"Join . . . who?" I said.

Andi had already put the pieces together. "You're not with the Watchers, are you?"

"I never said I was."

"But you let us think . . ." I dropped off.

"You are—" Andi hesitated, then continued. "You're with The Gate?"

He silently nodded. "Yes. And it is our hope that you will join us to help set your people free."

Chapter 11

Absolute silence. No movement. Except for the butterflies. I threw a look to Tank. He was definitely embarrassed, definitely numb. And definitely not looking up. Who could blame him? That had been quite a performance. Still, it was small potatoes compared to Bijan's statement . . . and his request.

Finally Andi turned to Bijan. "Do you have any idea what you are asking?"

"Yes," he said. "Of that I understand. Yet that was the purpose of bringing you here—in this place of peace and stillness—a place where you would experience your gifts more fully . . . and see the truth more clearly."

"So you've been lying to us about who you are," I said.

"For that I must apologize. But we saw no other way."

"And by 'we' you mean—"

"The Gate. Yes."

"And you expect us to believe what? That we've been working for the wrong side all this time?"

"I can only point you to the facts. I cannot make you believe them."

Chad spoke. "And by facts. . . You're talking about what we witnessed today. With our gifts."

"Not just from today, but please consider the evil you have witnessed these many months. Starting as far back at the Institute."

"The Psychic Institute?" I said. "Where you were doing all that stuff to those kids?"

"Those kids, as you call them volunteered . . . *freely* volunteered. They understood the sacrifice that had to be made—that *is* being made. Every day."

I snorted.

"Laugh if you wish, but that is the only way to liberate your planet from the oppressor's tyranny . . . and the evil of his people."

I wasn't buying it. Not for a second. But it did get me thinking back to my last set of visions. All that torture, and all that killing.

"What about the orbs?" Andi said. "The ones that followed us around and attacked us. Were they yours?"

"Of course."

"Not exactly friendly," I said.

"They are our eyes and ears. The enemy has spies everywhere. We are outnumbered two to one." Bijan turned to me. There was something in his eyes I'd not seen before. A depth. A sincerity. "And yes," he said, speaking more softly, "sometimes they are not so friendly. Sometimes their actions must be for our protection."

"*Your* protection?"

"To protect our identity. Our location. And sometimes, as you say in your sports, I am afraid the best defense is a good offense."

I frowned. He might have had a point. A small one. Maybe we had been intruding, accidentally threatening them. Or, in the Watcher's case, intentionally trying to destroy them.

Bijan continued. Besides his eyes, there was something in his voice I'd not heard—a gentleness, a soothing calmness. "You saw a glimpse of our beloved home, actually our home away from home, during your mind traveling exercise."

"The portal in the mountain?" Chad said. "The spaceship, the snowflake things?"

He turned those eyes on Chad and, I swear, you could actually see Pretty Boy's ego start to soften.

"Yes," Bijan said. "When your brain sees things it cannot comprehend, it turns such things into symbols."

Chad nodded, continuing to stare into his eyes.

"Those fairies were no symbol," Andi said. "Or that awful fungus."

"Or what invaded Chad in Vegas," I said. "And killed Stephanie."

Bijan gave a sad, heartfelt sigh. "Yes. But these were not of our making. They were His."

Cowboy looked up, his voice hoarse and quiet. "To try and stop you."

Bijan turned those understanding eyes on him. "Stop us from what?" His voice grew even more gentle. "Wanting to free you? We have nothing to gain, my big friend. What we do is only for you. It has always been for you."

It took a moment, but Cowboy was able to break

his gaze and look away.

"What about the professor?" I said. "He appeared to us, he told us we were in training."

"Yes."

"But not to fight *you*?" I asked.

There was no missing the hurt in those eyes or his voice. "No, of course not. He wants you to join him. To join us in fighting your enemy, our common enemy—this dictator who insists upon controlling all lives."

I took a deep breath. Like it or not, he was starting to make sense. And if what he said was even half true . . .

"Brenda Barnick." He smiled softly and it was like I felt some connection happening . . . way down deep inside. "Don't you understand? We are on your side. We've come all this way, we've made all of these sacrifices for *you*, to free *your* world. And you four— five, counting the professor—you are the ones, the special ones who have been chosen—"

"So he *is* alive," Andi interrupted. "I mean we've seen him and everything . . . at least we thought we have. But still . . ."

Bijan turned his smile upon her. "Yes, Andrea, and he misses you very much. He sends his deepest and warmest greetings to you in particular."

Tears welled in her eyes. "Can you take us to him? Can we talk to him?"

"Yes. That is our plan. He loves you. He always has." He turned to the rest of us. "In his own way he loves each of you all very much."

"And that file, the one he gave me?" Andi's voice was thick with emotion. "The one that only had a name?"

"Ambrosi Giacomo? Yes."

I leaned in, listened harder.

"He is our leader. Like each of you, he comes from a human mother. He understands your many struggles, your silent pain. More importantly, he fully experiences and feels your great bondage."

Andi started to nod.

"And his father?" Chad asked. "You say he has a human mother, what about his father?"

Bijan's face brightened. "He comes from a reality that is much higher. One that is far more understanding and compassionate than—"

"And he wants to overthrow God!" Cowboy had regained his strength. But with it his voice sounded harsh, judgmental. Not at all like Bijan's.

The same with Cowboy's eyes. They were full of anger. While Bijan's . . . I can't explain it, but the more I stared into Bijan's eyes, the more I felt a warmth, a soft blanket gently enfolding me.

He smiled sadly at Cowboy and tried to explain. "The name *god* is only a title. An office he has given to himself. Trust me, my big-hearted friend, there are many like your god, but they are much more benevolent."

I glanced to Cowboy. His chin jutted out. But he was so outclassed . . . and so wrong.

Bijan continued. "You say your god is good. Would such goodness allow so much pain and suffering in your world?"

Cowboy's face was getting red again. He forced himself to look away.

"Ambrosi Giacomo wants to free you from his tyranny." Bijan turned back to Andi. "And he wants you to join the professor in the battle."

Andi wiped her face and nodded.

He turned to me. "You saw the history, the death, the misery he brings."

"The thousands murdered," I said. "All in his name."

"Yes."

I felt the blanket tightening. So warm, so secure."

"Nearly two million," Andi said. "If you count the Inquisition, the Crusades, the witch hunts, that comes to nearly two million." She was understanding now, too. You could hear it in her voice, see it in her eyes. "Two million innocent people slaughtered in his name."

"Yes, Andrea. And if we don't stop him, there will be many more. So many more."

I was nodding now. So was she. I glanced over to Cowboy. His eyes were closed and his lips were moving. That's when I noticed the butterflies. I counted four. They were flittering about, faster than before. Probably my imagination, but they also seemed bigger.

"Bjorn?" Bijan called out to Cowboy, but the big guy never looked up. He just kept his head bowed and his lips moving. I'd seen him pray like that before. Nothing fancy, but sometimes stuff happened. Bijan continued to call, "Bjorn? Bjorn Christiansen."

No response. At least not to Bijan. Instead, I now heard Cowboy's voice. He wasn't praying, he was singing. I couldn't make out all the words, but he was definitely singing and getting louder.

And those butterflies? They were definitely getting bigger.

Bijan saw them too. "Bjorn, you must stop."

But Cowboy kept at it. The butterflies kept on growing. Pretty soon they were the size of crows. Flapping their wings faster and harder. We watched, awed and amazed.

Everyone but Chad. His eyes were still glued to Bijan. And his voice sounded like a little boy's. "And don't forget my gifts. All that hatred I read in their minds, in his followers. They're just his puppets, right? Power mongers who only want—"

But Bijan wasn't listening. "Bjorn!"

Cowboy's voice got louder. And now I could make out the words:

> ". . . waking or sleeping thy
> presence my light . . ."

The butterflies or crows or whatever they were flapped harder. And kept growing! They were more like eagles, now. Giant eagles.

"Bjorn, no!"

Cowboy finally looked up, his face filled with determination as he sang even louder. Loud enough for everyone to hear:

> "Be thou my wisdom and thou
> my true word . . ."

That's when all hell broke lose . . . or at least a sizeable portion of it.

. . . I ever with Thee and Thou
with me, Lord—"

Bijan tried to outshout him, his voice getting louder,
shriller. "Stop this! Stop this at once!" And the louder
it got, the more his face seemed to change. Not just
that gentle look of understanding, but his actual
features—his chin, his nose—everything about him
seemed to get longer, sharper.

And scales. At first I thought it was the light, the
flickering shadows from all those flapping wings. But,
no. His skin was actually growing scales, black and
shiny. Within seconds his face began looking more
lizard than human.

"Thou my great Father, I Thy true son . . ."

"Stop!" Bijan screamed. "I order you to stop!"

The butterflies that were the size of eagles had grown to the size of humans . . . and in some ways they even looked human. Except for those pounding wings. And the eyes on those wings. There were hundreds of them now. And they were real eyes. Moving. Looking around. Even blinking.

Bijan let loose a scream and I spun around to see him drop to the ground. He jerked and writhed like someone had thrown acid on him. "Stop! Stop it!"

But Cowboy wasn't stopping. Fact, he raised his arms and sang even louder.

"Thou in me dwelling, and I with Thee one."

"Brenda!"

Andi pointed to the winged things. They'd doubled in size and circled thirty feet above us, screeching and flapping their wings. One had all of its eyes focused on Andi. Another on Chad. A third watched Cowboy, but it was a lot higher up, like it was afraid to get too close. And the fourth? It stared directly at me . . . until it folded back its leathery wings and dove.

"Run!" Andi yelled.

Good idea, but where? There was no place to go. Except maybe to Cowboy. Like I said, those things seemed afraid of him as he stood there, arms raised, singing at the top of his lungs.

"Be Thou my battle Shield, Sword for the

fight."

Good enough for me.

I ran towards Cowboy as my personal monster screamed and came straight at me. It was close, but I got there, throwing my arms around the big guy's waist. The wing thing shrieked and veered off just as Andi's and Chad's started their attacks.

"Over here!" I shouted. "Hurry!"

No second invitation needed. They ran and ducked under Cowboy's arms with me. The things swerved off and circled, screeching in anger. And Cowboy? He just stood there, eyes closed, arms raised and singing:

> "Raise Thou me heavenward, O
> Power of my power."

"Help me! Somebody!"

I spun back to Bijan. He writhed on the ground looking more reptile than human. Like his face, his body had grown long and thin. He no longer had arms or legs, not even a neck. Just a face attached to something that squirmed and wiggled like a common variety earthworm. Or a snake.

Cowboy lifted his arms higher. Sang louder.

> "High King of Heaven, my victory won,
> May I reach Heaven's joys,
> O bright Heaven's Sun."

The winged things kept rising, pulling back like they were trying to get away. They flew higher and higher until one slammed into the stone ceiling. Not once, but twice. Like it wanted to get out of there. Like it *had* to get out.

A second one joined it. Then the other two. Again and again they hit the rock trying to break through.

That's when the roof cracked. Spider webs shot across the ceiling.

"Sssstop!" Bijan shouted. His voice and pleading as much hiss as words. "Sssstop thisssssss . . ."

Water began seeping through the cracks. A little at first. But more and more, until the rocks suddenly gave way. Then it was Niagara Falls. Niagara Falls with an avalanche of rocks.

"Cowboy!"

But even his magic couldn't protect us from the truck-sized boulders as they fell and splashed around us.

"What do we do?" Chad shouted.

"The wall!" Andi shouted. "Run to the wall and stay close to it!"

We took off. The wall was fifty yards away. Water continued falling, filling up the place as we sloshed toward it.

There was a sudden scream and splash to our left. One of the winged things lay there. Its head bloody and dazed. Dazed, but not dead.

I shouted at Cowboy, "Keep singing!"

He nodded and started up again.

"Be Thou my Vision, O Lord of my heart--"

By the time we got to the wall, the water was up to our thighs and rising fast.

"Now what?" I yelled.

Looking up we saw the wall had all sorts of rocks and ledges jutting out. There was only one and Chad gave it:

"Climb!"

And climb we did. The stones were wet and slick. I slipped more than once. So did everyone else. But not as bad as Chad, who fell all the way back into the water.

"Chad!" I yelled.

He popped back up, swam to the wall, and started over again.

It was rough going for all of us, even our resident jock. But we kept climbing—two steps up, one slip down, searching for the next handhold, pulling, slipping, scrambling. Water pouring all around.

We were fifteen feet from the top when my legs started to shake. Hard. Not because I was scared, but because they'd given out. I had no strength. They'd turned to rubber.

"Look!" Andi, who was just above me and following Cowboy, pointed downward. It was hard to see through the sheets of water, but another one of those winged things had been hit. Actually two. They were floating side by side, flapping in the water, trying to get airborne. But something about the water made it impossible.

I'm no mathematician, but three out of four meant there was one left. As I stood, hoping strength would return to my legs, I peered through the falling water and rocks. I eventually spotted it . . . forty or fifty yards away, almost eye level. So far, it had managed to dodge the crashing boulders.

"Look out!" Cowboy shouted.

I looked up to see the whole ceiling give way. Rocks, water, everything. I pressed myself against the wall as it kept coming down. A deafening thunder that went on forever and I thought would never stop.

But it did.

Well, at least the ceiling. But there was still the wall. Its edges were crumbling, caving in.

"Hurry!" Cowboy shouted.

I looked up to see him and Andi already on top. They were on their stomachs on what must have been the bank of the river, staring down at me.

"Miss Brenda, Chad, get out of there!"

I forced my legs, which still felt rubbery and strangely foreign, to begin moving. They did. They didn't like it, but they did. I was only a couple of feet from the top when I saw Cowboy's hands reaching down to me. I grabbed them and he pulled. I tried helping, scrambling with my feet, but he did all the work until I was up, over the edge and lying on my back, amazed I was still alive.

Chad came next.

But we weren't out of the woods. Not yet.

"We've got to get away from the edge," Andi shouted. "It's all going to cave in."

I rolled onto my hands and knees. Planned to crawl since I didn't have the strength to stand . . . until Cowboy grabbed me around the gut, lifted me and ran.

We'd gone twenty, thirty steps before the rest gave way. The entire wall circling the garden toppled, falling into the hole, smoothing it into a wide but shallow crater, a gentle depression, that slowly filled with the river's water.

Epilogue

"Is this seat taken?"

I pried open an eye. Andi stood in the aisle, laptop in hand. "Knock yourself out," I mumbled. To make room, I grabbed my coat from the seat beside me and winced in pain. There had to be a muscle somewhere that didn't hurt. I just hadn't found it yet.

"How many Advil this time?" she asked.

"Not enough." I stuffed the coat between my head and the plane's window for extra padding. "How long we been in the air?"

"Approximately ninety minutes."

I grunted, closed my eyes, and for the hundredth time calculated how many hours before I'd see my boy.

Andi started working her computer . . . for about

ten seconds.

"Hey there." It was Cowboy. "Kinda lonely up front. Mind if I take this here seat across from you?"

"Sure," Andi said. "No one's sitting there."

"That's swell." I heard him settle in. "Wonder what time dinner's gonna be?"

"Good question," she said.

"These headphone jacks work? Mine was broken."

Andi continued typing. "I hope so. Looks like we'll have some interesting movies."

"Fantastic. Kinda hard to find time to see them these days, with our schedule and all."

"Yes."

"Chad though, he says the hotel's got streaming video."

"Right."

"Just haven't gotten 'round to figurin' it out."

"Actually, it's quite simple."

"Yeah? Maybe you can show me sometime."

"No problem."

"Thanks."

And on they rambled—Cowboy looking for any reason to talk to Andi, and Andi too polite to shut him down. (Some things never change). We'd been through some pretty weird stuff and, like it or not, small talk always helped dial things back to semi normal.

It'd been thirty-six hours since we dragged our butts back from the river, caught some z's at Hotel Cockroach and managed to book a flight home. Not once had we mentioned what we'd just been through. Though I figured that was about to change.

I wasn't wrong.

"Miss Brenda," Cowboy called over to me. "You still getting all them strange visions?"

"Sleeping here," I said.

"Sorry?"

I kept my eyes shut, hoping he'd get a clue.

If he did, he didn't let on. Instead, he raised his voice, making sure I could hear. "Are you still getting all them visions?"

I shook my head.

"Nothin'?"

I sighed then mumbled, "I'm back to the normal ones—like what I sketch."

"That's what I figured. And you wanna know why?"

I didn't.

"Because what you were seeing in that cave, those other visions, they were all counterfeit. From the devil."

I opened my eye and gave him a look. "They were true."

"Of course they were true. That's how the devil works. He'll use 95 percent truth to get us to swallow his 5 percent lie."

"Right." He was dragging me into his conversation and there was nothing I could do to stop it. "So how am I supposed to tell the difference?" I said.

"Ain't that what these little missions are about?" he said. "Teachin' us to use our gifts?"

Andi joined in. "That's precisely what the professor told us."

"And we're learning stuff," Cowboy said. "'Bout the Gate, the Watchers and this Ambrosi fella."

"Least we know the good guys from the bad

guys," I said as I pulled the coat from the window and sat up. "But I've got to tell you . . ." I hesitated, deciding not to finish.

"Tell us what?" Cowboy said.

I shook my head.

He kept pushing. "What?"

"It's just . . . all that stuff I saw—the tortures, the murders. Ask me, there's not that much difference between the good guys and the bad guys."

"Except—" Andi motioned to the info on her computer screen. "This is the information you saw, the figures we discussed, correct?"

CHRISTIAN WORLD VIEW
Inquisition: 150,000 civilians killed
Crusades: 1.5 million civilians killed
Witch hunts: 50,000 killed
TOTAL: 1.7 million civilians killed

"Yeah," I nodded. "Pretty stinko."

"Yes," she agreed. "It's terribly incriminating."

"Except," Cowboy said, "none of that stuff was what Jesus wanted."

Andi shrugged. "Perhaps. But check this out." She brought up another chart:

ATHEIST WORLD VIEW
Stalin - Marxist: 20 million civilians killed
Hitler - Nitzche: 12 million civilians killed
Mao – Communist: 40 million civilians killed
Pol Pot - Communist: 3 million civilians killed
TOTAL: 75 million civilians killed

I looked at the numbers: 1.7 million verses 75

million. "Big difference," I said.

Andi nodded. "And that's not to mention the earlier mass killers like Tamerlane, Genghis Khan, and Ivan the Terrible. But look at this. The seventy-five million murders mentioned here that stem from an atheist world view have only occurred during the last eighty years. Compare that to the 1.7 million killed in over two thousand years."

I raised an eyebrow.

"Granted, even one killing is a tragedy and there is no excuse for it. But don't tell me the world is a better place without the God of the Bible . . . or the people who believe in Him."

I stared at the numbers. Andi definitely had a point.

"And don't even get me started on the creation of hospitals, charities, universities, public education, literacy, modern science, modern medicine . . . all stemming directly from the Judeo/Christian world view."

It had been quite a while since I'd seen her so worked up. And I'm sure she'd of continued if it wasn't for Chad.

"Hey sweet cheeks, what computer game you playing this time?"

Andi turned to me and slowly shook her head. I couldn't agree more.

"Hey, listen, smart mouth." (That of course would be me). "I'm getting word from your kid."

That got my attention.

"He wants you to hurry home. Says he's just ordered some pizza."

"Pizza?"

"Double combo, everything on it."

"We're not landing for another fourteen, fifteen hours."

"That's what I told him."

"And?"

"Said not to worry. He'll order more."

"Order more? How's he gonna pay—"

"5433 2209 3387 5822. Expiration date, 3-24."

"That's my Visa Card!"

"Kid's got a good memory."

"He doesn't know how to order—"

"Says he's been doing it every meal since you left."

"Every meal!"

"Practice makes perfect."

"Listen, you tell him, you got him on the line now?"

"Loud and clear."

"You tell him, there's gonna be some serious changes when I get home. You tell him that."

"Right." Chad closed his eyes like he was listening.

"Well?"

"Busy."

"Bus-"

"When he gets to playing his video games it's hard to hear anything over all the screaming, butchering and bloodbaths."

"Butchering and bloodbaths! I never bought him those type of—"

"#5433 22—"

"All right, all right!" I looked at my watch. "It's 4:10 in the morning there."

"Which is why he ordered pizza. Apparently all that killing really works up an appetite."

I swore and dropped my head back to the seat.

"Speaking of which, when do they serve dinner on this bucket?" Chad asked.

"Me and Andi, we were talking about that very thing," Cowboy said.

"Terrific. Hey, listen." Chad produced a large, spiral notebook. "I've been making a list of who did the most good back there. You know, kind of an MVP thing? And—anyway, you mind if I sit and go over my contributions? I probably missed a couple."

I groaned.

Andi forced a smile.

And Cowboy didn't miss a beat. "Sure, partner. Pull up a seat."

"Thanks, troll boy." He plopped into the seat in front of us, then pushed it back so he could talk through the gap. "I've got three pages so far, single spaced, but I'm sure there's more."

I gave another groan as he began rattling off his bloated accomplishments. By the sound of things we were just his supporting cast—extras in a superhero movie written, directed and, of course, starring the great Chad Thorton. I sighed, closed my eyes and tried shutting him out. But, of course, I couldn't.

It was gonna be a long flight home.

Soli Deo gloria.